Little, Brown Books for Young Readers

Hachette Book Group • 237 Park Avenue, New York, NY 10017 • Visit our Web site at www.lb-kids.com

Little, Brown Books for Young Readers is a division of Hachette Book Group, Inc.
The Little, Brown name and logo are trademarks of Hachette Book Group, Inc.

First Edition: September 2009

Hobbie, Holly.
Fanny and Annabelle / by Holly Hobbie.—Ist ed.
p. cm.
Summary: Fanny decides to make her very own picture book, starring her homemade doll, Annabelle.
ISBN 978-0-316-16688-1
[1. Dolls—Fiction. 2. Authorship—Fiction.] I. Title.
PZ7.H6517Fap 2009
[E]—dc22
2008045297
10 9 8 7 6 5 4 3 2 1

IM

Printed in Singapore

The illustrations for this book were done in pen and ink and watercolor.
The text was set in Cantoria MT, and the display type is handlettering by Holly Hobbie.

Fanny
& Annabelle

HOLLY HOBBIE

LITTLE, BROWN AND COMPANY
Books for Young Readers
New York   Boston

Saturday was drizzly and dreary, so Fanny decided it was an excellent day to make her very own picture book.

At the top of the first page she wrote *Annabelle's Adventure*. Annabelle was Fanny's favorite doll. Fanny had made her, after all. She didn't know just what the adventure was yet. She only knew Annabelle was going to have one.

"Here goes," she said.

Annabelle's Adventure
Chapter I

Annabelle lived in a cozy apartment with her delightful Aunt Sally. They were quite chipper and happy together.

"Good morning, Aunt Sally. It looks like a rainy day."

"Good morning, Annabelle. It's a grand day."

Guess what? Aunt Sally's birthday was coming.
Annabelle wanted to get her a golden locket with
both their pictures inside!

Annabelle counted all her money. Three dollars!
Enough to buy a beautiful locket.

Beginning the story, Fanny discovered, was easy. She hadn't even known about Aunt Sally until she wrote her name. She didn't know what Aunt Sally looked like until she drew a picture of her. The story just happened all by itself. Making a picture book was fun.

Annabelle's Adventure
Chapter II

Annabelle went to Bloominghill's department store. "I'd like to see a golden locket," she told the lady at the counter.

"I like this one." The lady smiled. "Isn't it lovely?"

"Yes," said Annabelle. "How much does it cost?"

"Let's see, this one is one hundred dollars."

"Well, I have three dollars."

"I'm sorry," the pretty lady said.

"We don't have lockets for three dollars".

Annabelle walked home in the rain.

Fanny was stuck. How would Annabelle get enough money to buy the golden locket? What if she just sneaked it out of the store? No, Annabelle would never do such a thing. Maybe she'd have to get Aunt Sally something else for her birthday.

What would happen next? That was the question.

Fanny decided to take a break from her story. She was thinking too hard.

"Mom," Fanny called, "can I go to Ted's Deli for ice cream?"

At the deli, Ted asked, "What are you up to today, Fanny?"

"I'm writing a story," she told him. "It's about Annabelle."

"That sounds like fun."

"It is," Fanny said. "But Annabelle has to buy a present for someone special, and she only has three dollars."

"How about she wins the lottery?" Ted said, winking.

"That's too boring," Fanny said. "It has to be exciting."

On her way home, Fanny spotted a pink envelope on the sidewalk. Ordinarily, she never picked up anything from the street, but this didn't look like ordinary litter. And it was pink.

The words *For You* were written on the envelope in bold letters. Peeking inside, Fanny caught her breath.

Tucked into the damp envelope were two new fifty-dollar bills.

Run, Fanny thought. *Run*.

The next day Annabelle was just walking along when she stepped right on a pink envelope. Inside she found a hundred dollars. Holy cow! Now she could buy Aunt Sally the golden locket after all.

But back in her room a strange thing happened. The longer Annabelle stared at all that money, the worse she felt. It wasn't really hers just because she stepped on it by accident. Whoever lost it was probably very upset.

At dinner, Fanny's mother asked, "How's that story coming along?"

"Annabelle has a problem," Fanny said.

"What kind of a problem?" her mother asked.

Fanny was bursting. Pulling the one hundred dollars out of her pocket, she said, "Look, Mom. It was lying right on the sidewalk. What should we do?"

"Yikes!" her mother exclaimed. "I suppose we should take the money to Ted's, in case someone goes there looking for it."

"I guess," Fanny agreed.

"Now what about your picture book?"

"I'm not sure how it ends," Fanny admitted.

"It's your story," said her mother. "Anything can happen."

Annabelle's Adventure
Chapter IV

Annabelle made a sign and put it on the front door.

If You Lost Some Money
Ring The Bell !

Soon there was a line of people at the door. But no one seemed to know anything about a pink envelope or what was in it.

"I don't think we can find out who lost the money," Annabelle said. "Everyone thinks they lost it."

"Well you're definitely the one who found it, my dear," Aunt Sally said.

Then it was Aunt Sally's birthday.

They went to the movies and then they
had hot fudge sundaes at the Big Scoop.

When Aunt Sally opened her present from Annabelle,
she said, "Heavens to Betsey, what a treasure!"
"It's real gold," Annabelle said. "And we're inside."

The End

But what about the real hundred dollars?

The very next morning, before Fanny took the money to Ted's Deli, she saw a girl poking around outside. Fanny went out to meet her.

"Hi, I'm Stephanie," the girl said. She was visiting across the street. "I'm looking for a pink envelope."

"You are?" Fanny asked. "Really?"

"It was my birthday present from my grandmother."

"Wait here!" said Fanny. And she went bounding up the stairs to get the lost envelope.

But that's still not the end of the story.

All weekend long another birthday had been coming—besides Aunt Sally's, that is. On Sunday, Fanny's mom turned thirty-five. To celebrate, they decided to go to their favorite restaurant.

"This is for you," Fanny said, presenting a wrapped-up package. "I was going to get something else, but I didn't have enough money."

"It's really about us," Fanny said. "I hope you like it."

"I think I'm going to love it," said her mother.